Pooh adore·ables READABLES

DISNEY
Lots of Pots

By Melissa Lagonegro

Illustrated by the Disney Storybook Artists
Designed by the Disney Global Design Group

Big pots.

Small pots.

Lots of big
and small pots.

Blue pots.

Red pots.

Lots of blue
and red pots.

Red paint!
Blue paint!

Lots of red
and blue paint.

Paint the pots
with lots of paint.

Big spots.

Small spots.

Paint the pots
with lots of spots.

Big pots.

Small pots.

Lots and lots
and lots of pots
with lots and lots
and lots of spots!

Here are the twelve
words you just read:

big   blue

pots   red

small   paint

lots   the

of   with

and   spots